remember me

remember me

by

Melanie Batchelor

A Division of Bold Strokes Books

2014

REMEMBER ME

ISBN 13: 978-1-62639-184-0

This Trade Paperback Original Is Published By
Bold Strokes Books, Inc.
P.O. Box 249
Valley Falls, NY 12185

First Edition: May 2014

Credits
Editors: Sandy Lowe and Cindy Cresap
Production Design: Sandy Lowe
Cover Design by Lee Ligon

Acknowledgments

I want to thank my family and friends for all their support, with a special shout-out to my fellow teen writers who have given me encouragement as well as advice. A huge thanks to my writing instructor, Mark, for helping me polish this novel as well as find the perfect publisher for it. And of course, I would like to thank everyone at Bold Strokes Books, especially Sandy, for her editing advice and patience with my newbie questions.

I know it's a cliché, but I couldn't have done it without you guys!

Dedication

For my mom, who was always by my side with support, advice, and coffee.

September
tore through the calendar
as if time were always meant
to flow this way.

Mementos of summer
gather atop my chest of drawers,
spread out
like an art show of our past.
Since August,
the value of the pieces
have all increased.

Today is
the aftermath
I was not prepared for.
How can I face
another school year
when everything has changed
so drastically?

I know that I have to move forward
but my mind is still stuck in summer.

LAST JUNE

•

The sun taunts us
from outside the classroom window,
gleaming of freedom,
the sure sign of summer,
while we review America's 19th century—
the Civil War, Lincoln, and
Manifest Destiny.

Mr. Williams is the only teacher
who still cares on the last day.
He wants us to write a review
on the battles and bloodshed spent;
the glorious people who got us from there to here.
He's a good teacher,
a passionate teacher.
I'll miss him
when sophomore year comes to an end.

Students glare at the clock,
willing time to fast-forward.
A few guys in the back joke about bikini season.
The girl beside me files her nails.
I study my notes.
They're filled with scribbles and timelines,
beginnings and ends of eras,
doodles of Lincoln and Carnegie.

When the final bell rings,
the ticking time bomb goes off,
and everyone races
to escape this place.

In my mind,
students jump,
flinging papers in the air.
They clap and sing and
congratulate each other on surviving.
Mr. Williams blasts "Another Brick in the Wall Part Two"
from an old boom box,
and we dance our way home to Pink Floyd.

But that sort of thing
only happens in movies—
a designed, deception of reality.
Here at Greenwood High,
we scurry to leave.

Forget about battles and bloodshed,
they think, pushing their way
through the door, past me.
I'm off to the beach!

Erica takes a drag of her cigarette,
decorating the clear summer sky
with clouds of gray smoke.

We hide away in Wildflower Park,
taking refuge on a rusty metal jungle gym.
She celebrates the end of the school year
with a pack of Marlboros.
I commend myself on mediocre grades
by sketching trees from the surrounding forest.

"I like it here,"
Erica says between drags.
"Thank God it's a forgotten paradise.
Can you imagine actual
'Mommy, I need this; Daddy, I want that' kids here?"

I continue detailing the trees,
drawing every inch of bark, every string of leaves.

"We've been here so many times
but we've never seen signs of life.
Even the birds have abandoned this place."
She grinds out her cigarette on the nearby slide.
She's slouched up against my side,
facing the parking lot while I face the evergreens.

Erica and I have come here after school
since the beginning of last semester.
Sometimes she brings a book,
but today she just has
tobacco, her thoughts, and me.

I used to come here
when I was little.
My parents would bring me.
Dad would push me on the swing
while Mom took videos as I screamed in delight,
"Look, Daddy, I can fly!"

I don't remember seeing anyone like us,
smoking and sketching,
when I was one of those kids
that Erica so dislikes.
Then again, maybe they were there all along,
and I just didn't care about anything more
than my newfound wings,
as I clung to the ignorance
of a six-year-old child.

Just like the rest of the town,
I forgot about this park.
It was old, rundown, and they wanted
an updated version.
But unlike the rest of the town,
I had Erica to reintroduce me.

"Wildflower is too peaceful for kids,"
I say, more to agree with Erica than
to express my own feelings.

Her black hair presses against my arm,
smelling of cigarettes and coconut shampoo.
"You think it's peaceful now,
you should see this place at night.
It's incredible."

We sit in silence.
She lights another cigarette.
I put the finishing touches on my forest,
inhaling Erica's distinctive scent,
just as addictive as nicotine.

I follow Erica to her house
in an attempt to spend
as much time as I can
next to her,
avoiding my own
lonely home.

She hates,
she hates,
she HATES
her townhouse.
The barred windows
and paper-thin walls
scream reality
and Erica is more
into fiction.

She digs in her jeans pocket,
then curses under her breath and
bangs her fist on the front door.

"Bea, I forgot my key!"

Beatrice Brooks was
Little Miss Beauty Queen in the '70s,
the go-to gossip girl in high school.
Now she's a cubical worker
and the foster mom of my best friends,
my only friends,
Erica and Asher Sinclair.

Inside the house,
the cold air touches me.
It's deadened and hollowed—
a bit bleak, a bit empty.

Corpses of forgotten items
decorate the hallway:
takeout cartons, deferred bills,
shreds of torn-up wrappers.
The air is still stale
when we enter her bedroom.
She lies on the bottom of the bunk bed.
I peer over the top
and see the sheets are made-up and clean.

"Doesn't Taylor sleep above you?"

"Oh, Bea kicked him out," she says.
"She hasn't gotten a replacement yet."

My hand shakes
as my fingers run over cotton

                                        I forgot
                                  these things
                                 could happen.

I sit on the edge of her mattress,
Not sure of what to say.
I'm not good at talking.

"Lie down next to me,"
she says.

This is one of those times
I wish I knew
what was running through her head.

Lie down next to me.
How much does that mean?

I want to do more than that.
I want to touch her,
kiss her,
be with her.

For now,
I lie down.

Asher
rolls into the room
on his skateboard.

His long black hair is
pulled back in a ponytail.
He's got one earbud in,
blasting Guns N' Roses so loud
I can hear it from Erica's bed.

"Ooh, am I interrupting something?"
My cheeks burn,
but Erica
is expressionless,
as if she's stone.

"Go away, Asher," she says.

He sticks his tongue out
like a child.
"It's my room too."
I giggle. I can't help it.

Erica is
less than amused.
In fact,
I'm not sure she heard him
at all.

I met Asher
the first time I came to their house.

"Hey, it's better than being locked in a closet,"
he joked (he always jokes)
when he caught me eyeing
their broken home.

Coming from upper suburbia,
I was surprised
this neighborhood existed
so close to my bubble,
the one I was always
trying to pop.

Erica glared at Asher.
I guess
she didn't think that memory
was anything to joke about.

Of course,
back then I didn't know
Asher was referring to their old life
with real parents
in a place that they once
called home.

The door swings open
as Asher leaves.
Sounds of life
creep through the open door.
The thud of pans falling,
a TV screaming,
a woman cursing.

The door's mouth closes
and swallows the sounds.
Walls keep in the quiet
and we lay
in silence

until Erica asks me,
no,
tells me, to go.
I pull on the metal knob,
hear the sounds of the real world.
I peer back at Erica.
She looks straight up,
eyes focused on nothing,
waiting for the door
                 to close
                 once more.

Angela Richards
is an accounting consultant.
Every day she dresses
in blouses of rich blues or purples,
a jet black pencil skirt,
and tops her façade off
with two-hundred-dollar heels and a Chanel briefcase.

As a child, she was
a victim of poverty,
a victim of a negligent family,
a victim of a shaky life.

She began her future
with a college scholarship,
then on to an entry level job
where she worked her way up,
further away from us.

Now she's a successful businesswoman,
the mother of Jamie Samantha Richards,
and lives in Greenwood, Virginia.

It all sounds
so perfect
on paper.

She's not perfect.
She's defective,
flawed,
human.
She's a widow,
his widow.
She's a mother,
my mother.

She's still
a victim
of this world
but the evidence
is harder to find.

I see myself
Spending the summer
listening to "Bohemian Rhapsody" with Erica,
laughing and joking with Asher,
with my sketchpad and pencil in hand,
drawing whatever happens to be
in eyesight or mindscape.
Asher hanging at the skate park.
Erica's dark green eyes.
Pieces of the forest.
Anything, everything.
Capturing these moments, these memories,
my version decorating
pure white paper.

My mom
sees things differently.
She wants me to join
a camp or a class;
some sort of constant activity.

"I don't want you wasting the summer away,"
she says as we walk down the cereal aisle of Superfoods.
Translation:
she doesn't want me sulking around the house,
friendless and alone
like last year.

I grunt in response,
and toss a box of Lucky Charms
in our shopping cart.
She puts it back,
and picks Special K off the shelf.

"You'll thank me when
you're a size two."

I wonder
if she'll ever learn
that I don't want to
turn my life into a schedule,
squeeze into doll-sized jeans,
or mold myself
to fill her stilettos.

Strangers
think the best of us.

I am The Average Teenager
with ripped jeans,
arms crossed over my chest.
Foot-tapping, gum-chewing,
not-quite-mature-yet.

She is The Caring Mother—
picks the healthy foods,
cell phone on fire with messages,
a genuine hands-on-her-hips
woman of conviction.

No scruff in the image.

I refuse to sign up
for a tedious class
or a patronizing camp.

Mom is not pleased.
Apparently,
I am missing out on a
"constructive" and "character-shaping"
opportunity
that would conveniently fit with
her work schedule.

It's too bad
we can never agree on anything
anymore.

Instead
I find a list of drawing exercises online
and pursue an activity
that I actually like.

LIST OF DRAWING EXERCISES

1) Draw someone or something that you miss.

I miss my dad.

Before the car crash,
I loved him,
but it was automatic.
Now I cling
to every memory of him,
not letting his leaf
fall from its branch.

I close my eyes and
smell apple pie.
I see Dad's strong arms
reaching in the oven and
unveiling his
freshly baked pastry.

I sketch him cutting
imperfect slices of dough
for the woven top crust
in the old kitchen
of our apartment in Ohio,
before Mom was successful
and Dad was still with us.

I redraw his face
several times,
scraping pencil and eraser over
the same area,
trying,
failing
to make it perfect.

My cell phone rings.
A steady *BEEP, BEEP, BEEP*
cuts through
my focus.

Hey J
Meet me in Wonderland

Second semester
Erica and I
were assigned as partners
for a psychology project.

It was about family relationships.
Go figure.

I'm from the
rich side of town.
I was supposed to hang out with
the overprivileged preps,
but they drifted away
when I met

Erica

when we found friendship through
our families' dysfunction.

She repelled the others
with cynicism.
I isolated myself
from the crowd.

Wildflower Park
has a run-down Wonderland essence.
It's the perfect place
to dream up a better life
or fend off a miserable one.

I spot the metal gate.
She's left it slightly open
like a private invitation.

When I walk inside,
I see her sitting on the gravel.
The sun gleams off her
skin like a spotlight.

She's staring at
an open notebook,
holding a pen in her hand
like a dagger
waiting to attack.

I sit across from her.
She doesn't look up,
just stares at
the first blank page.

"Jamie," she says.
It's a statement, a fact.
She told me to come, I came.
I always do.

She holds out her arms.
I scoot next to her.

She rests her head on my shoulder.

I feel
the familiar sensation
of a thousand nerves
exploding throughout my body.
A side effect
of her touch.

"I have this crazy idea,"
she says.
Her hot breath
traces my neck.

She swallows,
squeezes her eyes shut,
blinks them open,
and lights her cigarette.

She takes a drag
and begins again.
"I have this crazy idea
to write seventy pages
of poetry and prose
over the summer."

Words climb up my throat,
I want to know more,
but before I can say a thing,
she puts out her cigarette
and stands up.
"I've got to call Chris."

She walks away
and doesn't look back
or even say
good-bye.

He never went to Gym or Pre-Calc
so he has to repeat his junior year.
He looks like one of the Beatles
with his brown bowl of hair.
He'll bum a cigarette off her
if there's an audience.
He criticizes classics.
He says *man* and *like*
too much.

I have no idea what Erica sees
in wannabe '60s hippie
Chris Rush.

It was Chris's idea
to visit Virginia Beach.
"It's only, like, a couple of hours away,"
he gushed
not even bothering
to check the weather report
or give us more than
a day's worth of warning.

Erica, Asher,
Asher's girlfriend, Grace, and I
pile into Chris's truck.
I'm surprised he doesn't own
a freakin' punch buggy.

Erica rides shotgun.
She runs her fingers through Chris's hair.
I look out the window
and at my feet,
anywhere but
at them
together.

It's too cold
for swimming and tans.
I pull my
Greenwood High School sweatshirt
over my swimsuit
and sit in the sand.

I expect Erica
to lie down beside me,
                    quiet,
                        unblinking,
and read a novel
as thick as her arm
or maybe work
on her seventy-page project.

Instead I shiver
and watch
as Chris spins her around on his shoulders
and they dive into
the ice-cold water.

Asher makes his way
out of the ocean
and across the sheet of sand.

"What's wrong?"
He crouches beside me.

"Nothing."
I plaster on a smile.
Asher looks skeptical,
and I remember
I've never been good
at hiding my emotions.

"Come join us."
He smiles and
there's no question that he is genuine.
His hair is
dripping with salt water.
Goose bumps and sand
sprinkle his skin.
He couldn't look happier.

Grace calls his name
in her thick Puerto Rican accent.
I look over and see her
waving to her boyfriend.

I spot Erica and Chris
kissing in the water.

Asher stands up.
"Are you coming?"

Erica wraps her arms
around Chris's neck.
Their bodies pull closer together.

"I think I'll sit this one out."

He frowns,
then yells back to Grace,
"Hold on, babe, I'll be there in a second."

He sits down
and folds his legs like he's
meditating.

"So, Jamie," he says.
Erica and Chris are kissing.
                    kissing.
                    kissing.

"Does this antisocial behavior
have anything to do with
the crush you have
on my sister?"

For a moment,
I can't think.
My body feels
coated with ice.
Frozen solid,
all I can move
is my mouth
when I nervously shout,
"I uh, I um…I do not!"

Asher laughs.
"Oh please. You can't deny it.
You're brick red."

I bury my head
between my knees.
Damn.
Could I be any more
obvious?

"Don't worry," he says.
"I'm not going to out you
or judge you or anything.
I just…"
He looks out at the ocean.
"I know my sister, and
please, be careful."

Can you really be careful
when it comes to your feelings?
Is that even possible?
Can someone please teach me?

I nod anyway.
This seems to reassure Asher.
I relax when he says,
"Do you want me to splash Chris for you?"

LIST OF DRAWING EXERCISES

13) Draw a portrait of somebody you love.

I start with
the outline of
her heart-shaped face.
I compose
her crooked nose and
re-create
her acute eyes
as she's absorbed in a novel.

I express
every thick eyelash,
the thin scar under her
right eyebrow,
leaving no detail behind,
taking no artistic license
when sketching Erica's
perfectly flawed features.

"What are you drawing?" she asks,
her eyes still pinned
to the pages of her book.

"Um…the forest."

She snorts.
"Do you have some sort of
obsession with trees?"

I feel my cheeks burn
as I dip my pencil
into her rough lips.
"There are millions of ways
to draw the same thing, you know."

"Hmm, that sounds like something
I would say."

I smile,
feeling warm from
her approval.

Seventy pages.
She works on them
religiously.
She tells me she
sneaks off
to Wildflower Park
and writes until
a page is full.

"A page a day,"
she says,
"and it's got to be
perfect."

I want to know more,
but I leave it at that
because explanations
are almost never offered,
and if I pry for more,
she'll take the truth back
in an instant.

Mom has to travel for work.
"It's just a couple of days in New York,"
she says while applying mascara.
"Will you be all right on your own?"

Sure. Yeah. Of course.
Is there any other option?

She kisses me on the cheek
and says good-bye
before leaving to live her
briefcase, stiletto, fitted-suit life.

The house grows
when I'm alone.
The walls pull apart and
the floor stretches.

I tiptoe into Mom's closet.
Even though no one is home,
I'm scared that I'll get caught
holding on to a memory
she's forbidden from our thoughts,
or at least
that we don't talk about.

Under Gucci, Prada,
Chanel, and Wang,
I uncover an old hatbox
that belonged to my grandma.

I pull out
years of photographs,

each of them portraying
my dad.
Washing the car
or toasting champagne at his wedding,
he smiles in every picture.

I could never draw his image.
I could never capture that essence.

I lie on the closet floor,
the past pinched between my fingers,
my dad and I
building a sandcastle
four summers ago.

God, has it been that long?

Hey, it's Erica. Meet me at the library.

When?

Twelve o'clock tomorrow. I'm running low on stock.

I don't know if—

It wasn't a question. I've got to go, Chris is on the other line.

Oh.

Sunday is
Mom's mental health day.
She usually
combines Starbucks with reality TV
in an attempt to
take her mind off of
the papers that need to be filed and
the calls that must be made
come Monday.

I walk to the living room
and ask her
for her car keys.

"Absolutely not.
You're only fifteen!"

Why did I even ask?

"Fine, then can you
give me a ride to
the library?"

She sighs and
takes a sip of her latte.
"When?"

"How about now?"

She groans.
"Jamie, I'm not even dressed."

"It's not a fucking fashion show."

It just slipped out.
No control.
No conscience.
If I were theatrical
I would gasp,
slap my hand over my mouth,
beg for mercy.

Coffee slams
on the glass table.
Milky brown liquid
splashes from the rim
of the steaming mug.

"I'm not taking you anywhere!"

I storm up to my room,
then turn my head and see
Mom pressing her palm
against her forehead.
Mental health day
is officially over.

I'm sorry, I can't come.

What? Dammit.
You know I can't go alone.

What about Asher?

He's out with his friends.
And Chris is at work. Fuck.

Breathe, Erica.

I was depending on you.

I'm really sorry, but my mom—

I need you, Jamie.

…

I'll be there in half an hour.

I used to bike
with my dad.
He was the
outdoorsy type
and I
was eager for the wind
against my skin,
riding along
the paved road to
freedom.

The closest Mom gets
to nature
is when she has her monthly
mud mask.

I pull
my old bike
from the shed.
It's covered in
pink butterflies.
I can't believe
I ever went through
that phase.

"It's a piece of junk,
a hunk of metal,
a waste of space,"
Mom says
whenever we do our
spring cleaning.
"Let's toss it, Jamie."

But whenever
I see it,
I see him.

I think
she does
too.

I don't think
of how I must look
riding a
child-sized bicycle.

I ignore
the sweat running
down my back and
my heavy
breathing.

Erica
needs me.

It's rare
she does.

She laughs
when she sees me.
"Nice ride, J."

My cheeks burn
as I toss my bike
behind the bushes.

She slides her hand
into mine.
"Come on," she whispers
in my ear,
as if this simple trip
is a secret adventure
for just the two
of us.

She pushes the
front door open
and pulls me into
her world.

Erica
is the bravest person I know,
but even superheroes
have their weaknesses.

She loves
all things literary,
but she can't stand
to check out books herself.

"It's like buying condoms."
Erica pushes a stack of seven novels
into my hands.
"What I read is personal.
No one has the right to judge me."

Before I agree
to check out the books,
she has already
shoved me in line.

"Thanks, J," she says
and hugs my waist
from behind.

My heart beats so fast
I almost drop the stack.

"You can't just run off like that,"
Mom says
when I arrive home.
"No matter what."

I charge
into my room
and think,
hypocrite.

She knocks on my bedroom door.

"Jamie, please let me in."

I've been sketching furiously
and listening to my iPod
for an hour.
I'm not in the mood for this.

She sighs.
"If you ever want to talk,
well, I'm always available."

I almost laugh.
She hasn't been available
for four years.

Anger swells,
bitter and boiling.
I kind of *do*
want to talk…

but not with her.

Erica's not exactly
the listening type,
but I can rant
to Asher,
who will listen
without judging
until he's got me
laughing
instead of
raging.

From Lear Lane
to Good Hope Road,
to the left of Wildflower Park,
past Greenwood High School
and the neglected graveyard.

From gaudy mini-mansions and
white-collar professionals
to condemned buildings and
evicted families,
I bike to the Brooks residence.

Beatrice's red nails
curve along
the side of the door,
her fingers like spiders.

"Lemme guess.
You're looking for Erica?"
Beatrice says.
"Well, she's out somewhere."

"I'm actually looking for Asher.
Is he here?"

She pauses for a moment,
then rolls her eyes
dramatically.

"That boy, I swear.
I found weed and cigarettes
under his bed."

She picks at her nails,
as if this conversation
is some kind of gossip fest.

"Well, *I* don't want drugs in my house.
I had to call Social Services.
I swear, they're always
just like their parents."

Gone.
Just gone.
Leaving only the space
where he had once been.
Leaving only the pain
in my heart and my stomach.
She mentions him
for a moment,
a few words passing in an instant.

Asher.
Labeled Troublemaker.
Sent to a group home
like some of her others.

She says teens are like needles.
They pick, pick away at her...
except for the other Sinclair—
she's all right.
Quiet most of the time.
Always writing in some book of hers.

I check Wildflower Park.

She's gone.
Disappeared
just like him.

Gripping the sides of my sketchbook,
I try to picture something
different.
Something too good,
like the park at peace with life.
Wonderland, revised.

Maybe
just an image on paper
can make me feel better.

It's late
when I arrive home.
Really late.
Like, midnight.

I slip through
the back door.
I expect to find
Mom fuming in rage
or worrying,
or *something*.

Instead
she's at work.
Overtime.
Does she know
or even care,
if I'd ever
come back
"home?"

•

JULY

Erica, it's Jamie. I'm so sorry about Asher. Please call me back.

Erica, it's Jamie. What happened is awful. Do you want to talk about it? Please call.

Erica, it's me. Um, where are you? Are you avoiding me? Call me. Or don't. I'm just—I'm really sorry about Asher. Please call me back.

Erica, um, call me…when you're ready. I'm just—I'm worried about you.

The next week is spent in
solitary confinement.
I haven't heard a word from Erica
and Mom's away on business.

I read a book.
I watch too much TV.
I eat a carton of
chocolate chip ice cream.
I try to draw but
end up staring at
the pencil in my hand,
who used to be
my loyal friend
until my creativity
betrayed me

and now
my art
can do nothing.

My thoughts
create a wedge
between inspiration
and me.

Where are you, Erica?

I have a horrible habit
of spending these periods of time
when I'm alone
in Mom's closet
fishing out that old hatbox.

I try not to think about
my dad
below the ground.
I try not to think about
losing people
in general.

I'm sketching in the park
when Erica suddenly appears,
strutting through the gate into
Wonderland.

"I've changed my page quota
to fifty instead of seventy," she says
as she walks toward me.
"I just can't wait that long
anymore."

She looks the same
except her eyes
are inked creases in her skin—
melted and helpless,

or it might just be
shadows and sunlight
playing tricks on my mind.

I have to ask
when she sits next to me,
nothing in her hands.
No book.
No cigarette.

"It's been a week, Erica.
Where have you been?"

She picks at a
dirty fingernail.
"I've been hanging out
with Chris."

She turns and looks me
square in the eye,
and in that moment
I realize
she knows
that his name hurts.
And of course,
of course
she knows
that I love her.

And I'm
angry.

Why did she pick him?
Is it because of
his gender,
his looks,
his poseur personality?

Erica puts her head
on my shoulder.

I'm so
disgusted
with myself,
my exposure,
my desperation.

But
I still can't bring myself
to push her away.

And I agree
to be Erica's plus one
on a camping trip
Chris is hosting.

When Erica talks about it
she's so full of life,
like Asher's still here
and everything's all right.

We don't talk about him.
Or my messages.
Or what she was doing all this time
with Chris.
I don't tell her that I'm angry.
She doesn't tell me that she knows.

All we talk about is
the camping trip.
"A great escape,"
Erica calls it.

I'm eating dinner alone
(Chinese takeout)
when Mom walks through the door,
dragging a suitcase behind her.

"Jamie."
She muffles a yawn.
"I missed you.
How are you doing?
Hey, I got you something."

She digs in her suitcase
and pulls out
a wooden box filled with
drawing pencils.
The New York City skyline
is carved in the top.

"I was downtown
and saw this on display
in a little art store.
I knew you'd put it to good use."

She smiles and
hands me my consolation prize
for her absence.

Her attempt to buy forgiveness
is paper-thin,
clear as cellophane

but I'm glad at least she knows
how to bribe me.

Across the dinner table, Mom says,
"You know, if there's anything
you want to talk about,
you can always confide in me."

I'm still convinced
I can't,
but I'm curious.
Why is she offering again?

So I ask
and she simply says,
"Teenage years are hard.
It's nice to have a parent
to guide you through them."

I wish I had
both parents.

I wish Erica did
as well.

I meet Erica
in the park.
We wait for Chris
to drive us to the campground.

We talk about our favorite bands
and I offer her some of my
Starbucks latte.
I ask her how
her seventy—wait, *fifty* pages
are going.

"Right on schedule."
She looks at the ground,
not at me.

Right in the heat
of our discussion about Queen
I hear the park gate
rattle.

I look up and see
Chris shaking the metal.
"Come on, guys,"
he shouts from the entrance.
"My truck is waiting."

Erica hoists her duffle bag
over her shoulder
and I roll my suitcase
toward Chris.

I stare at him.
Feelings churn in my stomach
like stones.
Resentment and hatred
mix and groan.
This park is ours,
and he's
an intruder,
stepping on territory
that should be left private, alone.

I sit sandwiched between
Chris's friends.
Drake's body odor and
Jack's obscene hand gestures
make my legs squeeze together,
my arms cross against my chest,
my eyes search for a safe place
to land.

I try not to look
at Chris's hand on her thigh.
I try not to imagine
his hand being mine.

It's like the beach all over again.

Oh God.
Why did I agree to this?

The campground
is a tiny section
of a large community
of tents and fire pits
lined up like Levittown.

Stakes pile and
nylon tenting spreads
across a square of flat land.
Chris digs metal into dirt
while we tiptoe around
sheets of fabric
and ask him where
"the bendy things go."

Erica drops a metal pole.
"I can't do this.
Chris, babe, I'll kiss you
if you finish for me."

Of course he takes her offer.
Who wouldn't?

As I'm organizing tools,
I look up and find them still together.
I walk to their side of the tent and
drop my hammer.
Chris screams and
grabs his foot,
pushing Erica away.

Oops.

I don't let anyone
see my smile.

When we're done unpacking and setting up
(and Erica is halfway through a book),
Drake suggests a cigarette break.

Being the only one who doesn't smoke,
I crawl back into the tent
to get my sketchbook and pencils.

I turn around to leave,
but Erica is
kneeling behind me.

"Oh my God, you scared me."

She doesn't laugh
or apologize.

"Can I see that?"
She points to my sketchbook.
She's not really asking.
She never asks.
She expects.

I hand it over.

My heart races
and my palms get sweaty
as she flips through the pages
of my thoughts and feelings…

leisurely.

She passes through
a montage of trees,
my father,
the Greenwood graveyard.

A few pages later,
she sees herself.

Oh God.
I forgot about *that* drawing.

She stares at the picture
for a long time.
Minutes go by
and she sits
expressionless.

She begins to slowly
rip the page out.
I wince
but stay silent.
If she was anyone else
I would have snatched
my sketchbook back
in an instant.

"Can I keep this?" she asks,
pinching the drawing
between her fingers.

But she never really asks.

Through the flames
of the campfire
she sits with Chris.

         His arms
         hold her close
         around the waist.

Their legs
intimately
intertwine.

         Her hand
         cups his
         prickly chin.

Kiss
Kiss

         Why
         am I
         exhausted?

I'm almost asleep when
something brushes against me.
Erica is sitting beside me,
writing in her notebook.

I start to sit up, but
when she lies down
I sink back into
my sleeping bag.

She pushes her book
to the corner of the tiny tent.
"I didn't know you were awake."
She scoots in closer
so our noses are
practically touching.

Fresh raindrops
break the silence
and bounce off the tent.

The rain crashes harder,
and cold air creeps in.
Erica's icy fingers wrap around
the back of my neck.
Her eyes capture mine.
She leans in for a kiss.

Eyes closed.
Mouth open.
Fingers laced through
strands of hair.

Skin soft.
Chapped lips rough.
Stomach hollow
and exploding.

Holding on
to her, to the moment.
Hands and heart
afraid she'll let go.

Focused but
oblivious.
The need to breathe
is unimportant.

"Man, did you believe how *cold* it got last night?"
Chris peels a banana
as we eat breakfast
around the dead campfire.

"I know, man,"
Jack leers at me.
"I was about to make some heat
with one of these ladies."

Chris smacks him with the
banana peel.
"Just don't touch *my* lady."

The ghost of Erica's kiss
lurks on my lips.
I try to catch some
signal from her
that she's not *his* anymore.

I catch her eye,
but Erica's as closed as
her notebook.

And then it starts to rain.

It beats down so hard
and for so long
that we all decide
to dismantle the tents,
pack up the supplies,
and head home early.

Hey Jamie.

Asher! How are you?

Eh, I'm holding up.

How's the, uh—

It's not exactly the Four Seasons.

Aw, well, hey
we should all hang out.
I'll call Erica.

No, don't. I haven't talked to her since I left.

What? Why not?

Look, not all of us worship her like you do.
Sorry, Jamie.
Let's just say that Erica and I are sort of fighting.

Oh. Well, I hope you work it out.

Maybe we will—if she hopes so too.

Greenwood is relatively small
and predominantly Catholic.
It's no surprise that the only
place to worship in town
caters to the majority.

I doubt that Erica is part of the masses.
I just can't imagine her
praising a higher power.
So why did she ask me to meet her
in Greenwood Catholic Church?

My flip-flops echo
as I walk down the red runway
on the marble floor,
past rows of bare pews
and stained-glass windows.

Erica sits in the middle of the church,
arms crossed and legs resting on
the back of the next pew.

I take a seat beside her.
I say nothing.
She can fill me in
if she decides to.

"My parents are Catholic."
She looks straight ahead.
"So is Beatrice.
They say that they feel close to God in church,
that they feel His love and protection."

She throws her head back
and, in almost a childish way,
grunts, "It's not working for me."

It begins again
at ten p.m.

Exhilaration.
Want.
Happiness.

They move swiftly between
her lips and mine
as our kisses get faster and
rougher with passion.

I can
barely breathe,
let alone digest
that *I'm with her*,
that we're closer
than we've ever been before.
That Chris
isn't the one holding her.

I am.

"You look happy,"
Mom says curtly
when I slip through the front door.
She looks at the kitchen clock.
10:34.

"It's a little late to be coming home,
especially when I had no idea
where you were."

"I didn't think you'd be home."

"Why wouldn't I?"

Is she kidding?
She must think her office
is her home
and 13 Lear Lane
is the job she goes to.

I'm just a worker,
an employee,
a project.

"You're never home
until at least twelve."
I try to remain calm.

"I work to provide for this family."
Her toes dig into the carpet.
Her composure is on edge,
which makes me want
to give it one final push.

"What do you *provide*?"
I choose my words with care.

"Money! The necessities…"
She runs her fingers through her hair.

I wonder.
Is being a parent
a necessity for her?

Every night
I walk through the neighborhood
until I reach
Wonderland's gate.

Erica is always there first.
She writes in her
notebook
until I arrive.
Once she sees me,
she shoves it away
behind a slide or seesaw or tree.

She has a countdown
she always says to me.
"Only ten,
only nine,
only eight more days
before I'm done."

After that,
no words are spoken.

She leans against rusty playground bars,
writing in her notebook.
"Two more pages, two more days," she says,
while I lie down on the soft grass,
forming pictures out of clouds.

"Why are you doing all this writing?" I ask.
She clicks her pen a few times
and then replies slowly,

"Because…because I need to.
I love writing fiction,
but to be honest
I'm regretting the poetry."

"Why?"

I don't expect an answer,
but I can't help asking.
I'm so curious
about her.

To my surprise,
she takes a breath and says,

"Nobody asked us
if we wanted to be born into this world.
Nobody asked us
who our parents should be,
what kind of government we'd like for our country—
you know, how we want the world to function.
We are born with no options."

She pauses.
I flip on my stomach to face her.
She has that distant look again,
like she's lost in a thought
she's been carrying around for
far too long.

"It's like the world was a
blank canvas,
and as time went on
people painted a foundation,
then kept adding layer upon layer.
Sooner or later,
there were no spots of white left.
The paint has dried.
We can't change the past.
It's on the canvas. Permanently."

A rush of cool wind
shakes the trees
and leaves goose bumps on my skin.
Erica stares down at her notebook.

"I love writing fiction because
I create the world and everyone in it.
I can send them to hell or seventh heaven.
But poetry...poetry is too *real*.
In fiction,
I am God."

I watch Erica play God,
carving out the lives of her characters.
I wonder what drama she's throwing their way.
Is she starting wars and sinking ships?
Reuniting loves to a state of bliss?

Thinking about it makes me want
to read her stories,
but I'm even more curious
about her verses.

What is *too real* for Erica?

She stares at stars.
Leaning on my shoulder,
pointing out constellations.

"The bright one over there is actually Venus.
I used to think it was just another—
what's up with you?"

I look at her and smile.
"I'm just really, really happy."

She scrunches her eyebrows
like she's not sure what to do
with this information.
Then she snickers.

"Maybe you could teach me
how to feel that sometime."

I reach for the front door,
planning on disappearing
to the park with my sketchbook,
when I spot Mom watching her
Sunday fix of reality TV:
one of those Bravo shows.

Two women
fight to the death
over a *he said, she said.*

"Ugh, how can you watch this?"

Mom turns away from the screen,
obviously surprised to see me.

"It's entertaining," she says,
"and a great distraction from work, you know?"

I stare at my sketchbook.
"I guess so."

I walk to Wonderland
with sketchbook and pencils in hand.
The sight of the closed gate
makes my pencils fall from
shaking fingers.
I do the unthinkable:
I push the gate open.

Erica is here,
stabbing her notebook
with a pen,
grunting and crying and
writing.

"Erica?"

I can't believe it.
Erica cries?
Erica shows emotion?
Erica's vulnerable?

Erica stares at me
as if she can't believe I'm here,
witnessing
her humanity.

As if her empire is
crashing down.
A queen dethroned.
A fallen angel.

"Get out!"
she screams,

throwing her notebook
to the ground.
"Goddammit get out, get out!"

I don't know what
to do or say.
I stand rigid, fearful
of her fragility.
Erica's supposed to be
a force of strength.
She looks scared, shattered,
no longer the heroine
of my own fiction.

I don't know
what to do
except to turn
and walk away.

LIST OF DRAWING EXERCISES

30) Draw your future.

My future?
At ten o'clock tonight?
Wonderland and
intimate moments
with no mention of
foster care, the deceased,
or deadbeats?

Can tears and cursing
return to sweet and silent moments?
Will Erica still be in the park?
Will she leave
the gate open?

*Will ten o'clock
ever happen again?*

I open the hatbox,
the only place
my dad still lives on
in this house.

Dad's gone.
Asher's gone.
Mom's pretty much gone.

I don't want
to lose Erica
as well.

She texts me.
Remember, Wonderland tonight.
My body loosens,
my heart now
satisfied.

Again
Mom's long work hours
make night excursions easy.

I swing my bag
over my shoulder and
walk to Wildflower Park.

The gate is open.
Erica's gate.
Her control of when I come,
if I stay,
how long until I go.

I sigh, relieved at the invitation.

Her hands cross in front of her chest;
no tears or notebook in sight,
just a cigarette dangling from her lips.

"I'm done," she says.
"Fifty pages.
Fifty days.
I'm finally done."

I wrap my arms
around her waist,
congratulating her
and wondering if
I'll get to flip through
the pages.

When I pull back,
she's smiling.
Her grin's like a touch
of reassurance.
She doesn't seem broken
anymore.

"Come on."
She grabs my arm.
"I want to go somewhere
different tonight."

We've buried ourselves
behind layers of trees
so thick that
I can only see
the outline of
Wildflower Park.

"A little farther," she says
as she leads me through the forest.

It's warm tonight,
like summer's supposed to be,
but it's dark in the forest,
with only moonlight
to guide us.

"Stop," Erica says.
There's a white coverlet spread out
atop roots and dirt and leaves.
She stomps on her cigarette,
then rests on the blanket,
sinking into the pure white.

"Lie down next to me."

I do,
still wondering what it means,
still wondering
what pawn she'll play.

Wondering
if we'll ever reach
the endgame.

"It was my fault," she says
in barely a whisper.

I look at her.
Her eyes are focused on the sky.
I can't stop myself from asking,
"What do you mean?"

"It was mine,"
she says slowly,
as if her words stuck in her throat
like she's never
confessed something before.

She stops.
Coughs.
Closes her eyes.
That's when her words
catch fire.

"The weed. It was mine.
I got it from Chris."

What am I supposed to say?
I'm sorry?
It's okay?
Asher will forgive you someday?

She sits up,
leans over, and
kisses my lips.
I let her.
She pulls in closer.

I let her.
We roll over
and she lifts up
my shirt.

I let her.

She's got me
in a cosmic trance.
Stars, moon,
black sky
swallowing us
in the night.
Good-bye,
sunshine.
I am
a nightingale
soaking up
the pleasure of
celestial sex.

But

I stare at the stars,
wishing they were
clouds.
Light is
safe;
light is
comfortable.
The sun and I
know each other,
but the moon now feels
like a stranger.

Erica feels
like a stranger.

Silence
follows after.
Shell-shocked
silence.
The kind that makes
your skin transparent.
The type of
hush
that says too much.
The dead air
that makes you want
to crawl back out
the rabbit hole.

Then she says,
"I'm happiness-impaired."
A clamor in
the quiet sound.

I ask her what she means.
I'm surprised
I can use my voice.
The rest of my body
is paralyzed.

"I can't—I can't be happy.
I just won't allow myself
for some reason."

Crying?
Confessions?
Now feelings?
She's breaking all her rules.
She talks now, too much.
Telling me everything.
Her words cascade,
rushing, spraying
cold water drowning me.
I want to be
ignorant again
like at the beginning of the summer,
when Erica and I,
we were still
just an idea.
A fantasy that I never thought
would become reality.

Before her feelings and thoughts
became my burden.

"Jamie," she says,
her voice like air.
"It's time for you to leave."

After
she gave me her
secrets,
after
I gave her my
body,
she tells me
to leave.
She's *done*
with me.

"Jamie, please."
She starts to cry.
No sobs, no screams,
just streams of water
trickling from her eyes
in eerie silence.

I want her
to feel better.
I'll do anything
to make her better.

I start to sit up,
grab my stuff,
leave as she directed me
until…

Oh.
Oh.
Oh.

That's what I've done all along.

Giving in.
Giving her
my heart,
my hopes,
my want,
my happiness,
my body,
to manipulate.

"You used me."

"Yeah,
yeah, I did."

For the last time
I give her what she wants.

The gate slams shut.

Finished.
Final.

Forgotten.

AUGUST

I heard it
from Beatrice,
from the morning paper,
from Asher on the other end
of the phone.
But I first heard it
from my mother,
who said simply
late last evening,
"Oh, Jamie, did you hear?
A couple of hikers
found a girl in the forest
dead.
Erica something—
oh yeah,
Sinclair."

Today

I don't cry
like I'm supposed to.
I didn't cry
when I first heard that
Dad passed away too.

Mom still wipes tears away
every November 5th,
but of course she doesn't
talk about it.

She'll grab her briefcase with the
intention of leaving for work,
but she always stops at the
front door.
She'll slump back to her room
and won't appear until supper.

So now
I feel insensitive.
My best friend is dead
but I don't even
cry about it?

What comes out
of my mom's mouth
just doesn't seem possible.
It can't be,
                Erica can't be...

Tonight

is all wrong.

Ten o'clock
glares from my clock.
Tick, tock
Tick, tock
The minutes take too long.

My bed's no good
for sleeping in.
I walk to Mom's room,
sneak in her closet,
and bury myself
in a nest of blankets,
curling my arms
around that old hatbox.

Some type of poison
leaks into the night
that makes me think
of words like bells
ringing
        ringing.

I used to think
if you want to die,
just fall asleep.

Bark and branches
wrap
her porcelain
body
like a Christmas present.
Ribbons of blood flow
between trees.
Flesh melts
and decays into
nobody.
Skin cold, knife sharp,
slashes hugging
her wrists.

"Jamie. Jamie."

Mom nudges me awake.
My eyes flutter open
and she comes into focus.

She reaches for the hatbox
and takes off its cover.
I watch in awe
as she leafs through the photographs.

"I see you've found my secret stash."
She sits down beside me.

Her lips curve
into a weary smile
when she spots a particular
picture.

"I love this one."
She holds the shot of our family—
our *whole* family—
at a county fair in Ohio.

"I remember that," I say.
"It rained on and off the whole day,
but it was still so much fun."

"And I kept saying,
'Richard, honey, let's leave. It's freezing.'"

"But Dad and I refused to go—"

"—until you rode the Magic Dragon."

We grin at each other
until the moment turns gray.
Mom looks grief stricken,
and I can't help
but feel the same.

"Oh God," Mom says,
running her hand through her hair.
"It's so hard sometimes…"

"Mom?"

"Yes?"

"Can you stay home today?"

Sometimes
speaking
is as essential
as breathing
but far harder.
It's tough
to put emotions
into neat little sentences.

But sometimes

when there's no pressure,
there's no one asking
"Are you okay?
Would you like to talk about it?"
talking
is just as easy
as breathing.

> She doesn't pry.
> I tell her everything.

The service is held
in the Greenwood Catholic Church,
which I'm sure Erica
would have hated
but probably anticipated.

I abandon the azure morning
and step through the grand double doors
into a swarm of darkness.

The black
of Chris's stiff suit.
The black
of Beatrice's knee-length dress.
The black
of my mom's stilettos.
The black
of Grace's running mascara.
The black
of Asher's ponytail
hanging down his neck.

They stand together,
Erica placed
center stage.

Some part of me thought
Erica would be by my side
as if we'd watch another's funeral.

I even scan the crowd
for her eyes, her hair, her voice—anything.
But she's not settled with the living;
she's ashes in a faux wooden box.

I feel as if this
has only now
proven to be
real.　　•

Then

I dreamt of
an exclusive connection,
a special bond,
a real, public relationship.

I dreamt of
being a shoulder to cry on,
armor to wear.

Someone to rely on,
not someone to be tricked.

Now

I've given up on dreams.
I simply want
to survive this death,
to survive my hurt.

Survive this feeling
that I could have done
something more.

Right before
I slide into the passenger's seat
of Mom's Lexus,
Beatrice tugs at
my shoulder,
clutching Erica's ashes
in her other arm.

"I've got something for you."

I shoot a glance at Mom.
She turns the ignition off.
We're on
my schedule today.

Beatrice leads me to her sedan
and opens the back door.

"I don't quite know what to do with this."
She stares down at the ashes.
"I guess I'll just wait until
someone from Social Services
gets in touch with me."

"Here." Beatrice lifts another box
off the seat,
one of cardboard and masking tape.
"I think she wanted you
to have this."

"Are you okay?"
Mom asks
on the drive home.

For once,
I don't offer the
automatic answer,
the one that's easy for
the person asking
to endure.

Enough
of these questions.
They splatter like paint,
and cover up memories
with a thick layer of
mystery.

Enough.
I can't stand wondering
what she was thinking,
had she been thinking
about me? Asher? Chris?
About anyone?
Anything?

Did she bring me close,
then push me away,
with her thoughts only focused
on what she would do
once I left?

Once she was able to
do what she wanted.

The cardboard is so worn that it might as well be
made of paper. It's only about eight inches deep but feels
heavier than a small box should. I tilt it to the side. I'm
caught off guard when I see her all-caps handwriting

JAMIE'S.

I lock myself in my bedroom.
We have a staring contest, the box and I.
I'm scared of the unknowingness, yet intrigued
by another piece of Erica left to be uncovered.

The box taunts me.
Enough.

A half empty pack
of Marlboros
is what I see first.
A symbol of
the poster girl of smoke.

My sketch is
folded into fourths
and decorated with
creases and rough edges,
opened and closed
repeatedly by her fingers.
I caress the worn edges.

Hiding
beneath
lies her brown leather
notebook,
held together with a sliver
of thin rope.

There it is.

Fifty pages of
Erica Sinclair.

She left
a dot of paint
on earth's canvas
in the most
immortal way:
words in ink.

I guess that's how
she planned it.

Now her soul
sits in my bedroom.
What should I do
with the notebook?
Did she want me
to read it?
Is this my final chance
to know her?

What lies in these pages?
Poems of hardship?
Stories of death?
Words holding
candor
with a shaky breath?

Do I want to know?

I open
to the first page.
My heart leaps,
my fingers quiver.
I spot nine letters
jotted together
with thick black marker.

Publish Me.

I take a walk
but leave my sketchbook
at home.
My thoughts are too heavy
to carry anything else with me.

Once more,
even in death,
Erica does not ask.
She demands, expects.

Why should I publish this for her?
She used me—she hurt me.
She doesn't deserve it.

I keep on walking,
not sure where
I'm going
until I turn around
and wander into the forest.

I drop to the ground,
unable to walk farther.
I don't want to see
what became of that spot
the place where...

I lean against
the rough bark of the nearest tree
and close my eyes.
Could I kill the last
part of her?
No matter how much

I love her
I don't want
to be her.
      I don't want
      to hurt.

The journal
Taunts.
Frowns.
Glares.
It
burns
a hole
in my bedroom
where it sits,
waiting
to be read.

Will its contents
scar me
or cure me?
Leave me
feeling better
or worse?
The infinite possibilities
make my stomach turn.

I pick up the journal
and run my fingers
down the spine, over the leather,
then,
finally,
through the pages.

ERICA'S JOURNAL, FIRST POEM

To Fly

The world feels like air
when I escape the pressure of the sun.
Wide and rich and free.
At night, fantasy seems to unfold
and the world is open to interpretation.

Maybe I'll become nocturnal.
I can use the deep night sky
as the foundation
for my own world.
The moon and stars
will be my scenery
and the forest
will shield me from reality.

I close my eyes and
feel the cool wind against my skin.
My mind fills
with dreams of a sleeping sun,
not ready to rise.

Oh please, someone,
grant me the power to fly.

I'm curled up in bed,
back against the wall,
eyes glued to
the last stanza.

To fly...to fly.
Why do her words sound
more genuine on paper
than they did from her mouth?

She hurt herself far more
than she ever hurt me.
She was so jaded, so bitter,
she let that eat away at her.
I'm not sure if that's her fault
or everybody else's.
Everyone who ever bruised her.

Oh please, someone, grant me the power to fly.

Maybe
      I can.

I knock on the front door.
A young girl answers.
She looks younger than me—maybe eleven.
She crosses her arms and
blows a pink bubble from glossy lips.
"Who are you?"

Who are you?

"Um, my name's Jamie.
I'm…I was Erica's friend. Where's Beatrice?"

Bubble gum girl closes the door.
A minute later, it swings open again.
Beatrice is in the doorway
dipping a fork in a takeout carton.

"Sorry to disturb you during dinner.
I should have called…"

Mouth full of white rice, she says,
"It's just leftovers. Whatcha here for?"

"I've got something to ask you."
My stomach twists. I bite my lip.
"I want to talk to you about Erica's ashes."

She sticks the fork in the carton.
"Why don't you come on in?"

Beatrice and I walk to the living room.
We both take a seat on the under-stuffed couch.
I touch the polyester cushions.
I've never been this close to Erica's world.
She never let me.

"The ashes are apparently my responsibility.
The state will cover all of the expenses,
but I need to decide what to do with them.
If you have an idea, by all means, tell me."

I rub my fingers on the fabric.
"You know that box you gave me.
Her journal was inside, and as I read parts of it
I felt like…like I was in her head.
As if for the first time I knew
exactly what she meant."

I stare at Beatrice. She's tapping her foot, casually eating.
I don't want her to decide Erica's fate,
she barely cares, for God's sake.

"I'd like to spread her ashes in the forest."

Beatrice looks at me.
Why would you want to do that? her eyes ask.
But it doesn't really matter.
She now has the opportunity
to let Erica go.

I stand in the forest
with a backpack strapped
over my shoulders,
my flashlight shining
on the dark earth.

I don't have to do this.
I could scatter her right here.
That's all I signed up for.

But I'll let her fly—
not because I have to
but because I want to

and having power over that decision
makes me want to climb.

My fingers curve along the lowest branch.
The rough bark cuts my skin.
Deep breaths...now jump!
My legs hug the tree trunk.
I pull myself up, then rest.

It gets easier as I climb higher.
I use branches as stepping stones.
A gust of wind blows my hair back.
I pause, gripping the trunk until it passes.

I look for the next branch,
but all I see is the blackness of the midnight sky.
I unzip the front pocket of my backpack
and retrieve the small flashlight.
I grip it between my teeth
and continue climbing
farther from the ground,
higher in the sky.

I reach for a branch. It wobbles in my hand.
"Retreat, retreat!" a little voice in my head says.
But I can't, I'm already halfway there.

Looking down from the top of the tree,
Feeling the leaves and wind
brush against my skin,
I'm here, floating with the air.

The world feels like air...

A few nightingales flutter by my side.
I laugh. My voice booms through the forest.

...and the forest
will shield me from reality.

I'm invincible! Infinite! Dreamlike!

My mind fills with
dreams of a sleeping sun...

I pull out the box and take off the lid.
Once the next big gust of wind hits,
I toss her ashes and watch her fly,
specks soaring through the night.

...grant me the power to fly.

Seven days left of summer.

Asher calls me.
He turns eighteen next week.
Then he'll be gone.
"Cruising the Caribbean
and climbing Mt. Kilimanjaro."
I hope he really does.

"*Memento vivere,*" he says.
"That's my motto."

LIST OF DRAWING EXERCISES

42) Re-create a memory.

Wildflower Park
seems different
than before.
Not better.
Not worse.
Just not somewhere
I can call Wonderland
anymore.

I sketch a memory,
no, more like an era.
The "Jamie and Erica" series
summed up in a picture
of one girl drawing
and one girl writing.

I close the gate.
As I walk away
I see someone standing
at the edge
of the forest.

Chris Rush
stands alone.

He drops roses
from his fingertips.
I join him in
a shivering stillness.

"Oh, hi Jamie," he says.
"Um, I didn't know where to go...
I hear you spread her ashes here."

"Yeah, I did. But farther in the forest."

He stares at his sneakers.
"So what are you doing here?"
I hold up my sketchbook.

"Oh."

Silence creeps in,
an unwelcomed visitor.

"I'm sorry," I say.

He raises his eyes and catches mine.
"I'm sorry, too. For you."

I scruff my sneaker in the dirt.
"Yeah, well, I was just her friend."
I'm not sure
whether I'm lying to him
or finally being honest

with myself.

I turn away.
"You loved her,"
he says, like it was a known fact.
I guess there's no point
in denying it now.

"Does that bother you?"
I don't care much
either way.

He shrugs.
"Love sometimes, like,
overlaps between people,
you know?
You can't stop feeling."

"I should go."

"Wait—Jamie."
He grabs my shoulder.
I turn around.
His eyes are red.

"I think it was, like, really cool
what you did."

I smile, a weak little half grin.
"Good-bye, Chris."

Mom and I
go back-to-school shopping.
Binder? Check.
Loose-leaf paper? Check.
Pencils? Check.

I should grab a few
composition books.
I'll need one for World History
and Chemistry, for sure.

I'm trying to move forward,

but while I search for
black-and-white
marbled covers,
I spot
familiar
brown leather.

I walk over to the next aisle
and find Mom inspecting
a graphing calculator.

"Jamie, do you have a..."
she pauses.
"Is something wrong?"

"No," I say. "Nothing's wrong."
It's true. I'm happy even.
I've made a firm decision.

"Mom," I ask, smiling.

"Do you know of any good
publishing companies?"

SEPTEMBER

Today is
the first day
of another school year
I thought—*we* thought
we'd be sharing
with Erica.

Chris and I walk together,
backpacks hanging
from our shoulders,
wearing our school uniform
of jeans and a T-shirt.

I want nothing more
than to crawl back home
and hide behind
my sketchbook.
I bet Chris would like to
escape in his music.

We keep on walking,
listening to the wind flowing,
our mouths never moving.

That's what we do
for now.

We walk and
         keep walking.

About the Author

The first story Melanie Batchelor ever wrote was called *Cats and Dogs*. It was a five-sentence "book" constructed of printer paper and clear tape, featuring the misspelling of its own author's name. Fortunately, Melanie's writing has improved since kindergarten.

Melanie finished her first novel-length story at age twelve and wrote her second manuscript, *remember me*, at age fourteen. She has participated in several writing workshops and has met many talented teen writers along the way. Melanie is always looking to expand her knowledge, reading everything from young adult fiction to medieval history. She hopes to travel the world, open a used bookstore in the city, and write a bestseller—after, of course, she graduates high school.

Melanie currently lives with her family in Silver Spring, Maryland. You can visit her online at *www.melaniebatchelor.com*

Soliloquy Titles From Bold Strokes Books

remember me by Melanie Batchelor. After a tragic event occurs, teenager Jamie Richards is left questioning the identity of the girl she loved, Erica Sinclair. (978-1-62639-184-0)

Frenemy of the People by Nora Olsen. Clarissa and Lexie have despised each other as long as they can remember, but when they both find themselves helping an unlikely contender for homecoming queen, they are catapulted into an unexpected romance. (978-1-62639-063-8)

The Balance by Neal Wooten. Love and survival come together in the distant future as Piri and Niko faceoff against the worst factions of mankind's evolution. (978-1-62639-055-3)

The Unwanted by Jeffrey Ricker. Jamie Thomas is plunged into danger when he discovers his mother is an Amazon who needs his help to save the tribe from a vengeful god. (978-1-62639-048-5)

Because of Her by KE Payne. When Tabby Morton is forced to move to London, she's convinced her life will never be the same again. But the beautiful and intriguing Eden Palmer is about to show her that this time, change is most definitely for the better. (978-1-62639-049-2)

Asher's Fault by Elizabeth Wheeler. Fourteen-year-old Asher Price sees the world in black and white, much like the photos he takes, but when his little brother drowns at the same moment Asher experiences his first same-sex kiss, he can no longer hide behind the lens of his camera and eventually discovers he isn't the only one with a secret. (978-1-60282-982-4)

The Seventh Pleiade by Andrew J. Peters. When Atlantis is besieged by violent storms, tremors, and a barbarian army, it will be up to a young gay prince to find a way for the kingdom's survival. (978-1-60282-960-2)

The Missing Juliet: A Fisher Key Adventure by Sam Cameron. A teenage detective and her friends search for a kidnapped Hollywood star in the Florida Keys. (978-1-60282-959-6)

Meeting Chance by Jennifer Lavoie. When man's best friend turns on Aaron Cassidy, the teen keeps his distance until fate puts Chance in his hands. (978-1-60282-952-7)

Lake Thirteen by Greg Herren. A visit to an old cemetery seems like fun to a group of five teenagers, who soon learn that sometimes it's best to leave old ghosts alone. (978-1-60282-894-0)

The Road to Her by KE Payne. Sparks fly when actress Holly Croft, star of UK soap Portobello Road, meets her new on-screen love interest, the enigmatic and sexy Elise Manford. (978-1-60282-887-2)

Swans and Klons by Nora Olsen. In a future world where there are no males, sixteen-year-old Rubric and her girlfriend Salmon Jo must fight to survive when everything they believed in turns out to be a lie. (978-1-60282-874-2)

Kings of Ruin by Sam Cameron. High school student Danny Kelly and loner Kevin Clark must team up to defeat a top-secret alien intelligence that likes to wreak havoc with fiery car, truck, and train accidents. (978-1-60282-864-3)

Wonderland by David-Matthew Barnes. After her mother's sudden death, Destiny Moore is sent to live with her two gay uncles on Avalon Cove, a mysterious island on which she uncovers a secret place called Wonderland, where love and magic prove to be real. (978-1-60282-788-2)

Another 365 Days by KE Payne. Clemmie Atkins is back, and her life is more complicated than ever! Still madly in love with her girlfriend, Clemmie suddenly finds her life turned upside down with distractions, confessions, and the return of a familiar face... (978-1-60282-775-2)

The Secret of Othello: A Fisher Key Adventure by Sam Cameron. Florida teen detectives Steven and Denny risk their lives to search for a sunken NASA satellite—but under the waves, no one can hear you scream... (978-1-60282-742-4)

Andy Squared by Jennifer Lavoie. Andrew never thought anyone could come between him and his twin sister, Andrea...until Ryder rode into town. (978-1-60282-743-1)

Sara by Greg Herren. A mysterious and beautiful new student at Southern Heights High School stirs things up when students start dying. (978-1-60282-674-8)

Boys of Summer, edited by Steve Berman. Stories of young love and adventure, when the sky's ceiling is a bright blue marvel, when another boy's laughter at the beach can distract from dull summer jobs. (978-1-60282-663-2)

Street Dreams by Tama Wise. Tyson Rua has more than his fair share of problems growing up in New Zealand—he's gay, he's falling in love, and he's run afoul of the local hip-hop crew leader just as he's trying to make it as a graffiti artist. (978-1-60282-650-2)

me@you.com by KE Payne. Is it possible to fall in love with someone you've never met? Imogen Summers thinks so because it's happened to her. (978-1-60282-592-5)

Swimming to Chicago by David-Matthew Barnes. As the lives of the adults around them unravel, high school students Alex and Robby form an unbreakable bond, vowing to do anything to stay together—even if it means leaving everything behind. (978-1-60282-572-7)

365 Days by KE Payne. Life sucks when you're seventeen years old and confused about your sexuality, and the girl of your dreams doesn't even know you exist. Then in walks sexy new emo girl, Hannah Harrison. Clemmie Atkins has exactly 365 days to discover herself, and she's going to have a blast doing it! (978-1-60282-540-6)

Timothy by Greg Herren. Timothy is a romantic suspense thriller from award-winning mystery writer Greg Herren set in the fabulous Hamptons. (978-1-60282-760-8)